Ariella and the Talking Drum

Stephanie Coker Aderinokun

Layout By Levi Online Publishing

Cover Art By Godwin Akpan

Illustration by Ehiz Illustrates

Website www.ariellaandfriends.com
⊙ : @Ariellaandfriends

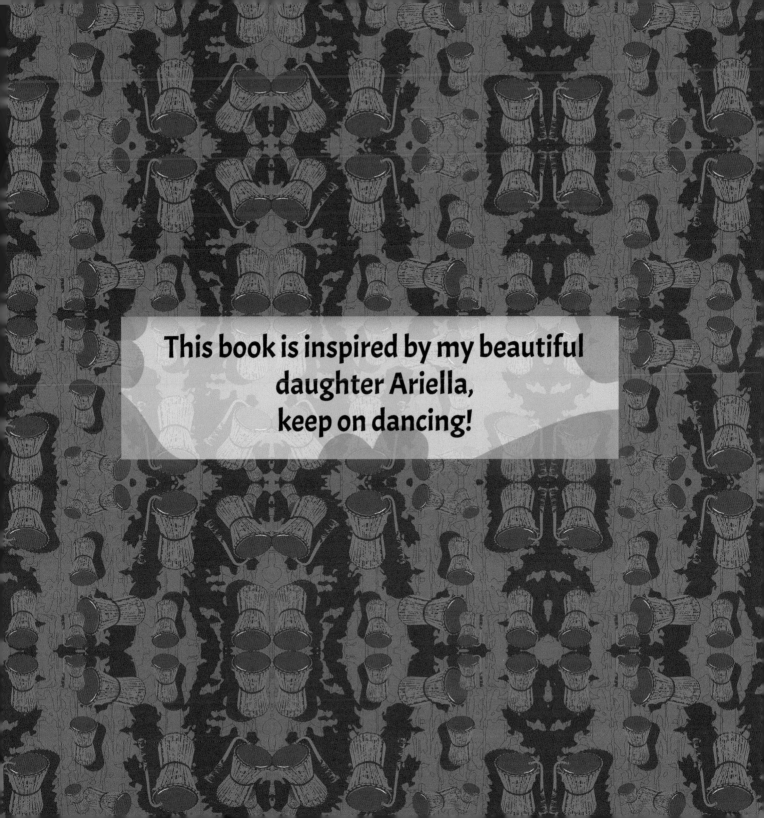

This book is inspired by my beautiful
daughter Ariella,
keep on dancing!

Ging gidi ba

bos bas!

What's that sound?

Olumo rock

It's Ariella and her talking drum, Tito.
They are the best dancing duo in town.

"Tito, we need to practice our dance
moves before we head to the Eko Dance
Competition. If we win, we'll get the
grand prize and become champions of
the dance floor."

"Says Ariella exictedly."

PARARARARA RARARARA

What's that sound?

rock

It's the palace guards.
What do they want?

Ariella! Princess Adeola asks that you hand over Tito, so that she can win the dance competition. In exchange, she will give you these beautiful coral beads, fit for a princess.

Hmmm…does the princess deserve Ariella's talking drum?

The guards are shocked and quickly leave.

Ariella and Tito go on their merry way.

They dance from street to street, until they arrive at the national theatre.

"Tito, we need to practice our dance moves once more," says Ariella. "It's nearly time for the competition."

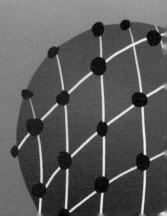

What's that sound?

Does Ariella **need** a dress to feel like a princess?

The maidens are shocked and quickly leave.

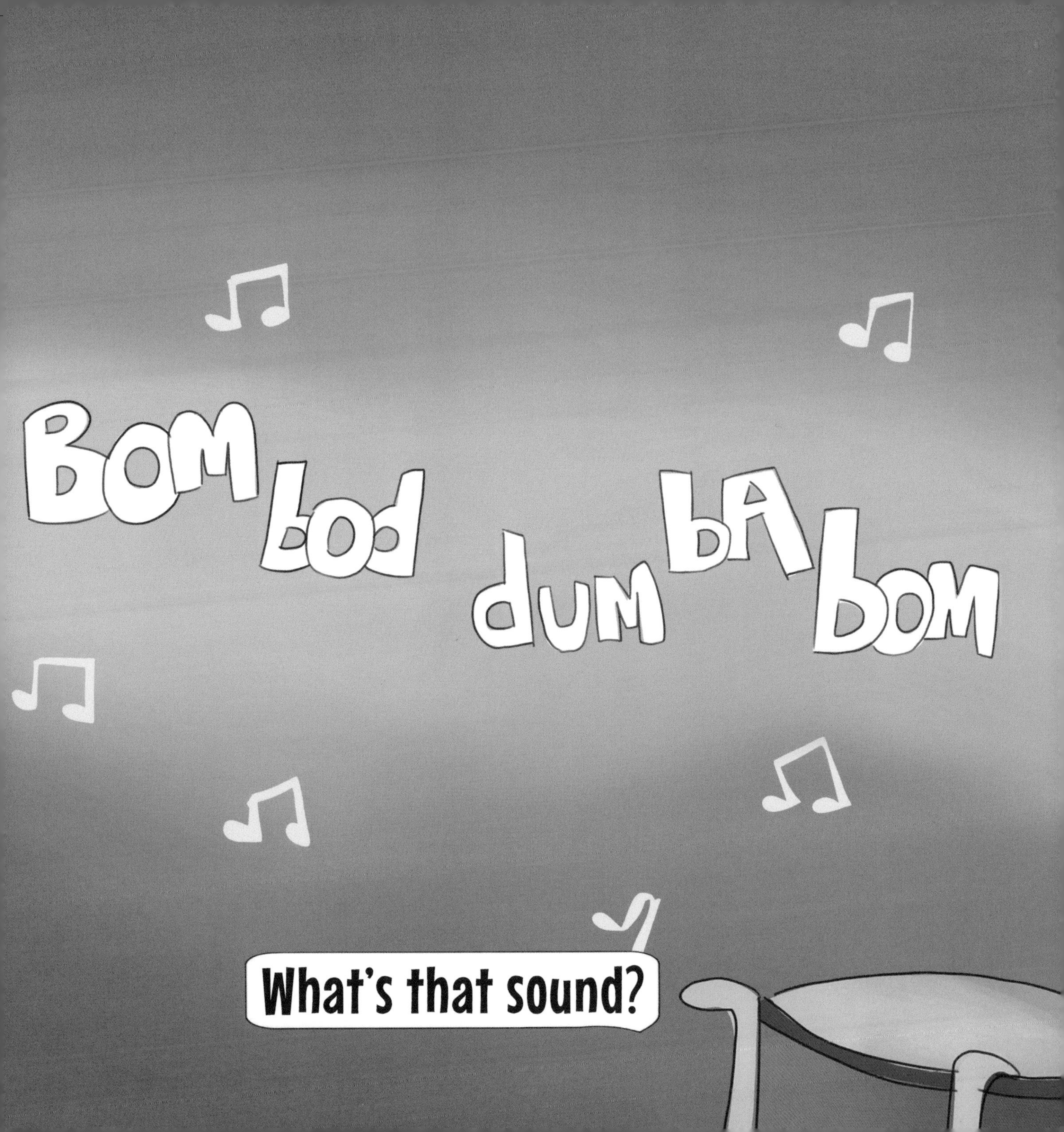
BOM bod dum bA bom
What's that sound?

Ariella searches high and low for Tito, but he is nowhere to be found.

Ariella is very upset.

She decides to go to the Eko Dance Competition.

Maybe she will find Tito there.

Ariella sees Tito with Princess Adeola on stage. But Tito is not dancing. Princess Adeteni gets cross.

"Why is he not dancing?" she yells.

Adeola gives Tito back to Ariella and apologizes.

"Tito let's hit the stage." Says Ariella.

Happiness comes from Contentment.

Says queen Adunni.

Ariella and Tito wow the crowd with their dance moves and beats, and win the Eko Dance Competition!

Hello,

I'm Stephanie Coker Aderinokun. I'm an award-winning British-Nigerian TV Presenter, Wife and Mother to a little foodie that loves to dance to a good beat. I have always loved storytelling. In primary school, I would write stories about imaginary friends back home in Africa as I hardly found stories I could relate to at my local library. The lack of representation of children of color in children's books inspired me to add to the small collection that now exists. I was compelled to write a story that showed the importance of being content as well as the importance of giving room to let other people shine. We are in a world that has increasingly made people feel like we need what others have and we often feel like what we have to offer isn't enough. I think this is an important lesson that should be learnt at a young age; to be happy for others, to shine and be content with what we have.

Printed in Great Britain
by Amazon